How To Make Your Life Really Count!

Subtitle: How To Upgrade Your Life, GUARANTEED, and

FIND TRUE PEACE ©

By Chris Briscoe

Published and by Copyrighted by

Chris Briscoe Publishers,

7th April, 2021 ©

Dedication:

I dedicate this book to my loving and devoted parents who gave me their best gift which was to love me.

I pray that they have come into contact with that greatest love and experience God, who is called Love because he is love, and know that his love is unending and a most personal and comforting love.

Preface:

WHY HAVE I WRITTEN THIS BOOK?:

This book concerns the greatest journey you and I will ever take; all of us are in the same boat, travelling along on this journey we call life. The reason I wrote these words in this book is to somehow try and reach out and help make your journey better. I personally cannot do that, but I know someone who can because he can do anything – that's why he's called God. I know that word "God" conjures up many emotions for some or maybe even no emotion, i.e. indifference, but can I invite you to give this God an opportunity to show you his power, particularly the power of his love; I mean, can I ask you to consider this?:

If there really is a God who is so powerful he transcends this universe, yet, this God has so much personal love for you, he wants to enter your life and show you that love in such a way, he will convince you that he is both all-powerful and good - good enough to have been the One who first thought of you as an idea in his mind, and who chose you and brought you into existence by the power of that personal love.

Yet, the problem is you just haven't experienced that love for yourself whereby his Spirit touches your heart and emotions and mind and floods them with the most profound but tangible feeling of peace and calm; and the power of God's love is powerful enough to control your circumstances in a good way and come into your life and bring to you the most wonderful, brand-new feeling like you are starting your life fresh and clean, with such a deep feeling of peace, beginning a real healing and fulfilment in your life and heart – your spirit - that maybe, you have been searching for such a feeling all of your life.

Maybe you cannot envision that such a Christian life holds the promise of adventure and the best life to live for you, however, later, when you look back in hindsight, I believe you will; foresight fills us more with the feeling of fear. i.e. fear of failure or fear that we are making a fool of ourselves, or dread that we are taking a particular step we feel is not what we prefer. But the good news is, once you have experienced God's personal love for yourself, then you will most likely realize that this Christianity does contain real power- the power of God's love for you personally; the fact that if you had been the only person living on this earth two thousand years ago, Jesus would have still come to this earth as a human to die a criminal's death for a very real reason - to take the punishment which you and I deserve for all those short-comings we have committed. This truth may make you feel uncomfortable or happy - that's the nature of truth! But like all truth, you can stake your life on it, but unless you test this truth, you will never know deep down; and wouldn't it be a tragedy if you didn't take up that opportunity to test this truth, and Christianity turned out to be true while you let it slip by you and you found out too late when facing the most desperate disaster of hell's flames?

You see, the reason you are holding back might be because you just haven't experienced this personal love for yourself.

Of course, hindsight is a better examiner of truth because experience is a better gauge of truth, to confirm whether we made the right decision or not.

But even for those who would still see value in not gambling on Christ, consider what you have got to lose? Consider the following which are words from the French 17th Century Mathematician, Blaiss Pascal wrote,

"Either Christianity is true or it's false. If you bet that it's true, and you believe in God and submit to him, then if it's true, you've gained God, heaven, and everything else.

If it's false, you've lost nothing, but you've had a good life marked by peace and the illusion that ultimately, everything makes sense. If you bet that Christianity is not true, and it's false, you've lost nothing. But if you bet that it's false, and it turns out to be true, you've lost everything and you get to spend eternity in hell."

(from Pascal's Wager, a section written in his, The

Pensées, 1682 by Blaiss Pascal)

Let me reword some of his words and add some of my own thoughts:

If Christianity turns out to be true, you would have gained heaven and God and all the riches of spiritual blessings, i.e. everything of worth, and you would have lost nothing; but if Christianity turns out to be false, then it would have just deluded you for a while, and you would have still lost nothing except your time and energies spent on Christian pursuits; only your pride might be hurt in that you believed in a cause which turned out to be false; Pascal regards that as time well worth spent because even though you believed in an illusion of Christianity which turned out false, at least you would have lived a life marked by the illusion of peace and eternal well-being and life.

But if it turns out that Christianity is true, think of the nightmarish circumstances you would face with the prospect of an eternal hell!

Therefore, Pascal is saying that since you would not lose if you believed in Christ and it turned out to be a false religion, at least you wouldn't lose everything as you would if you refused to believe and it turned out to be true, with the worst fate of suffering the eternal pain of hell's flames!

So, can you see, the other two alternatives are much better, i.e. believing in God, but then finding out it was false or believing in God and finding out that it was true?

So wouldn't it be more prudent to wager on Christ?

And whatever reason or stumbling block you erect or others erect to believing in Christ, maybe, the obstacle is you just haven't experienced the power of his love. And remember, the number one most probable reason, apart from man's pride, that they don't believe is because, they haven't experienced God's goodness for themselves, or they haven't been touched by his Spirit and his love. For God's love is a very real and present power and comfort, for you and I, and an abiding force which has to be experienced for yourself to be believed.

So why not wager, as Pascal exhorts us to do?

So, what I am inviting you to do is something both radical and audacious, yet if it results in your life and spirit experiencing a genuine spiritual encounter whereby you realize that God is someone who loves you more than anyone enough to be referred to as "Dear Father" then just think how much of a difference he can make in your life; and what is even more to consider: just think of what an amazing new life you could be missing if you refused to test

God's personal love out for yourself. Maybe, there are some of you reading, who would rather leave your life alone and continue on the path of non-committal. However, before actually deciding that, you need to consider the full consequences of what your committal or non-committal decisions means; I believe a useful exercise is to consider Pascal's Wager in this way:

Either God exists, or God doesn't exist.

You can live as if God exists, or you can live as if God doesn't exist.

Therefore, you have the following choices in your life:

1. If God doesn't exist, and you live as though He doesn't exist, you have no losses.

2. If God doesn't exist, and you live as though He does, you have no losses but gain the advantages of a more moral-driven life.

3. If God does exist, and you live as though He doesn't, you lose

EVERYTHING!

4. If God does exist, and you live as though He does, you have no losses yet gained
EVERYTHING!

Now living as though God exists involves far more than just acknowledging that He exists (as the Bible warns us in James 2:19: "You believe that there is one God. Good! Even the demons believe that and shudder." NIV Bible). It must involve a recognition of the need for God's forgiveness in Jesus Christ.

Pascal wrote, in his The Pensées,

"God is, or He is not. But to which side shall we incline? Reason can decide nothing here. There is an infinite chaos which separated us. A game is being played at the extremity of this infinite distance where heads or tails will turn up. What will you wager? According to reason, you can do neither the one thing nor the other; according to reason, you can defend neither of the propositions."

"Do not, then, reprove for error those who have made a choice; for you know nothing about it. "No, but I blame them for having made, not this choice, but a choice; for again both he who chooses heads and he who chooses tails are equally at fault, they are both in the wrong. The true course is not to wager at all."

"Yes; but you must wager. It is not optional. You are embarked. Which will you choose then? Let us see. Since you must choose, let us see which interests you least. You have two things to lose, the true and the good; and two things to stake, your reason and your will, your knowledge and your happiness; and your nature has two things to shun, error and misery. Your reason is no more shocked in choosing one rather than the other, since you must of necessity choose. This is one point settled. But your happiness? Let us weigh the gain and the loss in wagering that God is. Let us estimate these two chances. If you gain, you gain all; if you lose, you lose nothing. Wager, then, without hesitation that He is."

"That is very fine. Yes, I must wager; but I may perhaps wager too much. Let us see. Since there is an equal risk of gain and of loss, if you had only to gain two lives, instead of one, you might still wager. But if there were three lives to gain, you would have to play (since you are under the necessity of playing), and you would be imprudent, when you are forced to play, not to chance your life to gain three at a game where there is an equal risk of loss and gain. But there is an eternity of life and happiness. And this being so, if there were an infinity of chances, of which one only would be for you, you would still be right in wagering one to win two, and you would act stupidly, being obliged to play, by refusing to stake one life against three at a game in which out of an infinity of chances there is one for you, if there were an infinity of an infinitely happy life to gain. But there is here an infinity of an infinitely happy life to gain, a chance of gain against a finite number of chances of loss, and what you stake is finite."

(From, "The Pensées", in the Section, "The Wager" by
Blaiss Pascal, 1862)

Here Pascal is saying that if there is a fifty/fifty percent
chance of gaining or winning, someone might wager his
own life to gain two more lives after he has died since there
is an equal risk of gain or loss, i.e. 50/50, but if you had the
chance of gaining three more lives for one life, you would
be imprudent to not to. But even more than that, since here
we are talking about an eternal life of living forever which
carries great loss if we don't wager yet nominal risk of loss
if we do and it turns out that Christianity is false, then, it
would be stupid not to wager.

And Pascal makes the point that since we are already on
this journey called life, it is not optional to just opt-out of
choosing and just remain in the abstention camp.

As Pascal pointed out, one must wager - he wrote,

"It is not optional. You are embarked. Which will you choose then?"

Therefore, if you have any pre-conceived conceptions of God or religion which may normally stop you from taking that step of faith – any stumbling block – genuine or construed - which stops you from inviting God to show you the power of his love, can I ask you to lay down for the purpose of this experiment of testing God's personal power of his love for you?; and also, if you are really, deep down, searching for truth and a definitive answer as to whether there is a God who transcends this universe, who because of his personal love for you, has the power to make all the difference in your life, then please can I invite you to pray the prayers at the end of Chapter Two?

Thus, when you have received the greatest revelation for your life, that you are loved by the most incredible and unending love, this love will never let you down as long as you place your hand in his hand; thus, think of all the incredible blessings which are headed for you, when you trust your heavenly Father and seek him; when you apply his promises to your life that he has promised to make those promises a reality in your life, upgrading your life no end!

This book was written to remind us that there is a world of wonder and adventure waiting for you inside you and outside you; but the problem is we are all born spiritually "dull" because our spiritual receivers or antennas need repairing first; it means we cannot discern God in our natural self; when Christians ask us to pray or read the Scriptures to us, it's like they are speaking a different language to us; well, in a sense they are because those words were written by the Spirit of God and without the Spirit of God inside us, they seem alien. That's why it's so important to first get the Spirit of God inside us. Before we can communicate or interact with God, we first need to ask God to come into our spirit and repair our spiritual antenna which is broken, which was broken from birth because we were all born with broken spiritual antennas in need of repair by He who made us; as we inherited that spiritual equipment from Adam who was the first to allow it to be broken; but the good news is that God has provided a way for your spirit to be regenerated, or born-again when you ask Jesus to come into your spirit; thus, when you believe in Jesus and when you receive him by faith, then God sends his Holy Spirit and performs a miracle in your heart, and your broken spirit is repaired - that part of you which can discern God and communicate with Him - your spiritual antenna.

The truth is, until our spiritual antennas are repaired by a supernatural touch of his Spirit, we remain blind - spiritually blinkered, just like racehorses we might look successful but we don't know where we are going.

To truly meet God, we need his Spirit to come down and enter our spirit - but for that to happen, we need to believe in the Son, Jesus Christ and receive him into our heart, by his Holy Spirit.

John, one of Jesus' disciples wrote,
"He was in the world, and though the world was made through him, the world did not recognize him. Yet to all who did receive him, to those who believed in his name, he gave the right to become children of God— children born not of natural descent, nor of human decision or a husband's will, but born of God.
(John 1:10, 12-13, NIV Bible)

Did you notice that John tells us that in order to become his child, we need to do two things?:

1. We need to receive him, i.e. Jesus.

2. Believe in his name, i.e. Jesus' name as my personal saviour who died for me, yet also, rose again from the dead, and now, as I dedicate my life to him who is my Lord,, everything I say, or do is a reflection of my relationship with him.

So this is one of the reasons why so many people struggle with believing God because their spiritual antennas/ receivers are broken and need repairing, as to know God we need the faculty of our regenerated or born-again spirit because without that we cannot discern God as he is spiritually discerned.

That is what the Bible tells us,
"The Spirit searches all things, even the deep things of God. For who among men knows the thoughts of man except his own spirit within him? So too, no one knows the thoughts of God except the Spirit of God. We have not received the spirit of the world, but the Spirit who is from God, that we may understand what God has freely given us. And this is what we speak, not in words taught us by human wisdom, but in words taught by the Spirit,

expressing spiritual truths in spiritual words."

"The natural man does not accept the things that come from the Spirit of God. For they are foolishness to him, and he cannot understand them, because they are spiritually discerned."
(1 Corinthians 2:10a-14, New International Version Bible)

Elsewhere in the Bible, in the book of John, Chapter Three, there is a story of a Jew called Nicodemus who was a ruler among the Jews, a politician as he was a member of the Jewish parliament called the Sanhedrin. He visited Jesus at night because he had a number of questions. He probably visited him at night because he was afraid that he would be seen with this Jesus, who to the Pharisees and Sadducees was viewed as a "little upstart". Nicodemus had questions for Jesus about how can a man enter the Kingdom of God:

He asked Jesus, "Rabbi (teacher), we know you are a teacher who has come from God. For no one could perform the miraculous signs you are doing if God were not with him."

In reply, Jesus declared, "I tell you the truth, no one can see the kingdom of God unless he is born again."

Nicodemus replied, "How can a man be born when he is old? Surely, he cannot enter a second time into his mother's womb to be born!"

Jesus answered, "I tell you the truth, no one can enter the kingdom of God unless he is born of water and the Spirit. Flesh (your natural birth) gives birth to flesh (your natural birth) but the Spirit gives birth to the spirit. You should not be surprised at my saying, 'You must be born again.' The wind blows wherever it pleases. You hear its sound but you cannot tell where it comes from or where it is going. So it is with everyone born of the Spirit."
(John 3:2-8, New International Version Bible, with words in parenthesis by C.J. Briscoe)

Did you notice in the above passage the word "spirit" is sometimes spelt with a capital "S" and sometimes a small "s"? This is to distinguish between our spirit who we are born with and God's Spirit who is God himself in Spirit.

So as we have read, Jesus told Nicodemus that he had to be born again, and this was a spiritual birth not a physical one so he needn't have to return to his mother's womb, yet his spiritual antenna needed to be repaired and regenerated by the Spirit of God; and the same is true for you and I. This is important if we are to understand spiritual matters, if we are to progress from thinking in mere earthly terms, and progress to the deeper or heavenly thinking - the language of the Spirit, if we are to get a much wiser perspective instead of being mere babes who think about everything through the prism of mere material values or the Natural Law. There is another law at work called the Spiritual Law which is far superior and to which this Natural Law is accountable to, to which you and I are accountable to. From whence comes those faculties we have each been endowed with, such as our conscience, those meta-physical faculties we have which tells us and convicts us with an uncomfortable feeling when we have done something wrong, or when we have not done something we should have done; mere atoms and physical electricity are too dull to tell us such things, because a law far superior to the Natural Law is convicting us of wrongdoing - a law which was written and inspired by God himself, and which without the Spirit coming down and writing that law on your heart, you remain spiritually illiterate. Without which, you may look like you have everything together in the natural world, but wait what happens - woe and betide, what will happen when, one day, all that physical treasure, comes crashing down around you, which it most definitely will, and must definitely crash, one day.

So if you want to be born again, and live a life devoted to God, experiencing his great power, then you need to believe in his Son, Jesus Christ, and receive his Spirit into your heart, if you have not yet. Without which, we remain blind - spiritually blinkered, just like racehorses we might look successful but we don't know where we are going.

But What Does Grace Mean?

In the First Chapter of John's Gospel he writes in Verse
Seventeen,
"For the law was given through Moses; grace and truth
came through Jesus Christ." (NIV Bible)

As you probably already know, Moses gave to the Jewish
people "the Law" what was later called the Torah or the five
books of "the Law", i.e. Genesis, Exodus, Leviticus,
Numbers, Deuteronomy which are the first five books of the
Old Testament of the Bible.

But Jesus Christ introduced an entirely different concept,
not of The Law or the Law of Sin and Retribution
administered by Moses, but of grace and truth, where,
because of his undeserved favour upon you and me, he
took the retribution and punishment we deserve in order to
appease the God of justice because justice includes both
judgement and mercy. Yet, there is a subtle difference
between the meaning of mercy and grace,
i.e. Mercy means not having what we do deserve =
    JUDGEMENT.
    Grace means receiving his mercy and gifts which we

do not deserve because
of Jesus' sacrifices =
FREE GRACE.

So Mercy means "Not having what you do deserve", i.e. punishment for all the times we lied, stole or misrepresented God and ourselves and others; while grace means, "Having what we don't deserve, i.e. all or any of God's gifts".

 I want to just spend some time talking about grace because it is not always familiar to contemporary minds, i.e. the concept of Biblical grace.

But what does that word "grace" mean? In today's language people use it differently, for example, "You can dance very gracefully" or "This skater's routine is very graceful."

But the word grace means, "Receiving favour which you do not deserve, necessarily."

Let me show you an acronym which might help you to

understand what grace means:

God's
Riches
At
Christ's
Expense.

So what I am trying to convey is that the grace of Jesus Christ is given to us freely, but this grace was not achieved at no cost; the cost was to Jesus Christ on the cross. So this grace is free but it's not cheap.

Our freedom came at great cost to Jesus.
Grace is free, but it is not cheap.

So, to be a true follower of Jesus Christ means we are so conscious of that great debt of love we owe to Jesus in dying for me and you, individually, so that even if we were the only person living on this Earth, he would have still come and died for us, personally; because he knows your name and thought of you as his idea, and chose you to reveal this amazing personal love for everybody and anybody; therefore, we just want to serve him for the rest of our lives.

The Law Came Through Moses

The Law of God including The Ten Commandments was given to Moses who introduced it to the people of Israel. Moses led Israel out of Egypt in 1513 B.C. when he was 80 years old, so he was born in 1593 B.C.

He lived to be 120 years old who died in 1473 B.C.

Grace and Truth Came Through Jesus

Jesus was born in the fall of 2 B.C. 1591 years after the birth of Moses, but 1471 years after Moses died.   So first came the Law introduced by Moses, but around one thousand-five hundred years later, Jesus introduced the grace and truth of God.

So, mercy means "Not having what you do deserve", i.e. punishment for all the times we lied, stole or misrepresented God and ourselves and others; while grace means, "Having what we don't deserve, i.e. all or any of God's gifts".

Inside this book I hope you will find out how you can receive all of God's gifts to you.

Chapter Two.

MY TESTIMONY.

This is What I Experienced When I Became a Christian,

i.e. My Testimony I Would Like to Share with You:

To know God, we must first experience him, because His Truth is Revealed not Learned.

The concept of God and trying to convey the concept of God can be tricky - I mean tricky in the sense that people can so easily be put off by religious jargon and spiritual terminology. The tricky part is communicating how practical and refreshing having the Spirit working in our lives can be - like experiencing a breath of fresh air every hour when the Spirit speaks to our spirit and communes with us every day. The only way I know to achieve that is to tell you what I have experienced myself, and what I have learned.

In the year 1987, I became a follower of Christ. Yet, prior to that, as I had been born in England, I had always thought that I was a Christian because I had thought, mistakenly, that being born in England made you a Christian; until then in 1987, I found out the truth that being born in England didn't make you a Christian as much as going to Macdonald's Hamburger Restaurant didn't make you a hamburger, or just as going to church didn't make you a Christian as much as going to KFC made you a chicken; so when I filled out a form, under the question, "What is your religion?" I would always write, "Church of England," or "C of E" until, in 1987, I realized that was a wrong concept, for true religion isn't about a denomination like Church of England, but rather a relationship with Jesus Christ where he becomes the most important component, the number one ingredient in my life, i.e. the linchpin which smoothes out all my problems when I hand them over to him; because then my problems become his problems, and his shoulders are much wider than mine and he knows what to do with all those problems and how to overcome them, because of the fact that he is always sitting on his throne, so everything, including all problems has to submit to him, and this is empowering when we experience this truth for ourselves.

As for me, at the age of 19, I found a supercharger for my life called the Holy Spirit who, in case some of you don't know, is the third person of the God-head theologians call the Trinity; once he connected with me, then I experienced what I can only describe as a supercharging power for my life which meant my entire perspective on life changed and it was like physically I was transferred from the doldrums of the deepest valleys of despair to the heights of ecstatic joy, when I received Jesus Christ by the power of his Spirit filling my own spirit; quelling all my fears and tears, and giving me the one commodity which most people are pursuing but few find until they allow his Spirit to deposit into them his physical peace; I can't tell you enough how that feels to you, all I can say is when the Holy Spirit imparts to me his Holy peace, I feel the greatest comfort, joy and peace, and then, I catch glimpses of the depths of his love for me.

If you have never experienced that for yourself, then you will, no doubt, find it difficult to understand what I am talking about, because these words concern the language of the Spirit and Spiritual matters, which mere flesh or our natural mind cannot understand; but the good news is you will understand when you become born-again of your spirit, when God the Holy Spirit fills your spirit and makes your dormant spirit come alive, which is called being "born-again" when his Spirit regenerates your spirit and you are regenerated with his life – when God turns everything in your life the right way up, and so you see the world the way he sees the world governed not by mere Worldly laws but by the Kingdom of God, where the power of his love overcomes every problem. And once you receive that unconditional and unlimited love in your spirit then you can love your enemies with that same love, and you can love God and love yourself with that same love, you can forgive by an act of your will just as God chose to love you and me by an act of his will.

Now I was able to give someone all my burdens and worries, and exchange them with my own love and allegiance, and receive the most profound yet real and tangible peace; because his shoulders hold up the universe, he was able to hold me up and pull me through my circumstances when, on my journey of life, I faced the harshest of circumstances, because his shoulders were big enough. When I met the one person who I have experienced to be my greatest comfort in my distress, the greatest alleviator in my stress, and the greatest enabler, the greatest peace-giver and comfort-giver, to give me power to overcome. And because then, I had someone to pray to and surrender all my heavy burdens and distress to, my health, my well-being - both my mental and physical as well as spiritual health went from strength to strength.

And when I experienced his overwhelming peace, I began to feel the feeling of what it feels to be satisfied that someone bigger and greater, and more capable than me was on my case and working on my behalf to move heaven and Earth, or rather to bring heaven to Earth through my faith connection and begin to see all the cobwebs of my life disappear.

I don't know if you believe in God or not. But this book is to help anyone who is struggling to believe. Some people don't believe in God because they can't see him, which is a valid reason until you realize that you don't need to see him to believe – you can discern him with your other faculties, like in your spirit and in your feelings which God the Holy Spirit will reveal to us.

While for others, they don't want to know him and they would refuse to believe in him even if God visited their bedroom, tonight, unless he convicted them of their great need of him by his Holy Spirit penetrating their stubborn, cold hearts, when the Spirit showed them his great, personal love, and they were moved to repentance.

As for me, God himself has persuaded me that he is alive in my life personally, and this is a story of how he did just that. I wrote this to tell you my experience; maybe some of you dear ones don't believe in God, well that's your prerogative, but if ever you need help in believing, God's your man, or rather Jesus Christ is your man. And the best and right way to get that ball rolling in that direction is to just send a prayer up to him asking for help, asking him to show you that he is alive, and not just alive but alive in your life, personally in such a way that, even if you were the only person living, he would have still come and died for you personally. As long as that prayer you send him is sincere and has even the smallest measure of faith, then he will answer you. And if it's faith you need, he has even promised to give you that as a gift, from the book of Ephesians, Chapter Two,

"For it is by grace (his unmerited or undeserved good-favour) you have been saved, through faith - and this is not from your own effort of good works - it is a gift from God, so that no one can boast."
(C.J. Briscoe, Updated English Version, of Certain Scripture Portions)

You can pray either or both of the two prayers which follows at the end of this chapter, i.e. Chapter Two:

Some people don't believe in God, but as for me, I cannot help believing when God has brought into my life so much evidence of his invisible hand. I have believed in Jesus Christ for 34 years this year, and I can say, he has been the greatest source for upgrading my life, ever. I have "uncountable" instances in my life when God intervened in my life in such an amazing way with his amazing grace, there is no way I could put it down to co-incidences.

So 1987 was the first time I felt the profound touch of God's Spirit upon every part of my being; and I found that one power that alone can give me real peace, which is a peace that you can feel in your deepest emotions and mind; that was when I found the greatest love found in Jesus Christ; 34 years ago - writing, now, in 2021 - I found the one power that can sever all the cords of frustration and death in my life. I have been a Christian for 34 years, and I can honestly say that having the greatest power which is God's love residing in my heart and emotions, means I have always had a rock, who is called, "The Rock" which I can lean on when my life implodes and when every other strength crumbles; and since I gave my life to Jesus in 1987, I have never looked back, although there were times of great suffering when I questioned God's love, i.e. when I found it difficult to reconcile what I was suffering with God's personal love when I wondered why God didn't seemingly do more for me if he loved me that much. I realize now that the truth was more that I didn't pray enough or have faith enough or just that God was doing something deeper in me through his discipline.

Those kind of questions which, to be honest with you, are still outstanding, yet because of the amazing future God is bringing into my life, such questions about past suffering I prefer to remain in the past, because such concerns are eclipsed by the amazing greater awareness of the multiple blessings I am enjoying now and I am about to enjoy. Thus, I am sure I can leave those questions and every question with God, and so can you leave every question and concern you have – even any misgivings you may have in putting your faith in Jesus with God, and in time, he will reveal the answer to those questions, if not now, most definitely in eternity, when he will reveal everything hidden.

My Relationship with the Concept of Church and Religion Began a Long Time Before My Conversion

Although as a young boy I had attended church during my elementary years, it was only on the pretext of earning some pocket money as a choir boy. I had never heard about the real radical power of the Gospel of Jesus Christ, through the Holy Spirit of God, certainly not in the high Anglican Church I was attending as a choir boy, and it would take more than a sincere Anglican priest to penetrate a boy's heart whose motive to be "in a church" was to earn "a bob or two". I had heard that Jesus had died for the world, but I had never heard before I was nineteen-years-young, that Jesus died for me personally; I had heard the message, Jesus died for the sins of the world, but certainly not for my sins, to such an extent that if I was the only person living on this Earth two thousand years ago, or even now, he would have still come and died for me.

So my real journey of faith began at the age of 19; my twin-brother, Paul, had been talking to me about Jesus, as he had just returned "to the church" after his spell in that same Anglican church singing as a chorister next to me where we were paid a few minor pence to turn up for practice during the week, but where we were paid, in my memory, forty-five pence to sing at a wedding on Saturdays, while a weekday practice was three pence and a Sunday matinee or evening-song came in at thirty pence; but when we sang at two weddings, it amounted to eighty pence, which was a good amount of money at a time when one penny could buy you a piece of paper-wrapped bubble gum.

During that conversation, Paul had said to me, "Did you know, Jesus died for your sins?" I had heard in the Anglican church that he had died for the sins of the world but not for my sins. Paul invited me to attend his newly found church - I said I would give it a try with an "open mind". So when my brother invited me to his pentecostal church which belonged to the "Apostolic church movement" he had been attending for around a month, it sounded radical because it looked like it was taking over my brother's life, but I reasoned that if it gave him some peace of mind, it was doing his health good.

So I decided to take up my brother's invitation, and on that first visit when the worship service started, I noticed that the members in the congregation sang in a very different way from those who sang in my old Anglican church back in my home-town of Horsham. They were singing their songs with such a passion and they were beaming with such joy over their faces as if they really believed the words they were singing, that attracted me to them and this church – what struck me was the way they were singing with all of their heart as if they believed the words that were coming out of their mouths - they were mostly singing choruses not hymns, not that I have anything against hymns, but the choruses were sung with such passion and truth, it attracted me to them because of the substance of them singing from "truth" with hearts that were "truly on fire". I realized these people thought about Christ as the Lord of their entire life, not just so called "Sunday Christian" which I subsequently realized is a misnomer. I am not saying that Anglican Christianity is just Sunday Christianity, but what I began to realize was the actual Christianity of the Bible which talked about being born-again was a radical life where Jesus is Lord of all or not Lord at all, wasn't an American brand of Christianity but rather was straight out of the pages of the Bible and confirmed and sealed by God the Holy Spirit - not just with words from a dusty book, but with the confirming power of God the Holy Spirit, confirming his promises from the Bible, and his personal love for me.

Yet, I didn't come into that true church of Christ - which isn't a building or an organisation or a denomination but a person - without first being pulled by the Devil and his cohorts as well as at least one man who looked to be "an angel of light" to me at the time, but who turned out to be a diversion.

A few months before "returning to church" which was actually my first encounter with the true church, the true body and representation of Jesus, I had been struggling with how to find inner peace myself, and I happened to "stumble" upon a book in the local bookshop called, "His Healing Hands" written by someone who had what he described as "a gift" which he believed was given to him by God or by "the Governor" as he referred to "God". In this book he describes that when he laid hands on people who had been afflicted, they had come away feeling relieved; whether physically or just emotionally, I don't know.

Yet, what struck me as a great flag of caution was some of these same people drew pictures which were shown in the final chapter or at the end of the book, that later, after being prayed over by this man, they had felt the urge to draw pictures, and that they had felt those pictures were not controlled by them but inspired by another power. However, it was only after becoming a Christian that those drawn pictures threw up concerning flags because they were probably, most likely, inspired by an infiltration of demons or a demon who had been able to get into these poor and unsuspecting individuals through the laying on of those "healing hands" from the, just as unsuspecting man, who those hands belonged to, who I believe, even though he was acting sincerely with his own "good faith", I believe he had, himself, been deceived because he was not being controlled by the Spirit of God, as his books did not contain any reference to the Gospel of Jesus Christ. I wish that man no ill, in fact, I have prayed for his salvation while writing this Chapter, but the Bible does warn us against such things:

"For such people are false apostles, deceitful workers, masquerading as apostles of Christ. And no wonder, for Satan himself masquerades as an angel of light. It is not surprising, then, if his servants also masquerade as servants of righteousness. Their end will be what their actions deserve."
(2 Corinthians 11:13-14, New International Version Bible)

At the time, 34 years ago, it just so happened that the author of that book lived locally, so I climbed into my car after writing a letter to the man telling him that I had read his book and that I wanted to visit his "clinic".

I drove my car to one of the surrounding villages to try and track the author's "clinic" down. I had the address, as given in the book for his "clinic", which was located next to the home- address, I believe.

I remember, now, that I couldn't find the exact address so I called into a village-shop and asked for directions. Eventually, I found the place, I parked my car and walked up the gravelled path and knocked on the door. A lady of middle age or beyond answered, I said words like, "Hello, excuse me, I have a letter here I would like to deliver, please."

She took the envelope with a "thank you", and closed the door.

So about one week or two weeks later, I received a reply which was a handwritten note telling me that if I would like an appointment, then I could call the following number.

But as God's providence had it, or rather as his deep kindness has it, a few weeks later, while I was contemplating what to do with that letter, I had that conversation with Paul, in our kitchen, while one lady - an elder's wife who was kind and full of God's love and full of his Spirit who was in the sitting room, who had been helping Paul, but now, Paul and I were talking in the kitchen as I prepared a cup of tea or coffee for us all.

So when I did take up the invitation from my twin-brother to visit his church, during the worship, one of the other elders at the front said that they felt somebody was here who might want to know more about this Christianity, and if that was me, to speak to one of the leaders after the worship service.

So after the church service, I met with another elder, Mike, and his wife who was the same dear lady, Coral, who had been at my brother's and my house for a tea and a chat, her name is Coral; she said to me words such as "If you decide to follow Jesus, this Christian life is the greatest adventure you will ever live!" I had gone into that Church thinking Christianity was just another religion among many with a list of "Do's" and "Don't's," but only when I actually decided to try Christianity did God begin to blow away all my misconceptions.

Coral knew that I had been contemplating going the other way of not following Christ but following that other man, so she strongly warned me that I had to choose one or the other, but definitely not both. So I said to Coral and Mike that I will decide to attend this Church with an open mind. After attending that Church a few Sundays, I realized they preached the whole Bible and they were obviously Bible believing, Bible-carrying-in-their-hearts Christians who regarded Jesus as Lord of every minuscule decision as well as major. I thought at the time that if this Christianity really has the power to make me a new person with a new hope that can never leave me, then I will give my life to Jesus. Therefore, I decided to keep attending that church and listening to the sermons; and the message I kept hearing was that Christianity and the life of faith was all or nothing, I had to make Jesus Lord of all my life, or he wasn't Lord at all. I had to come to that place where I committed my life, and my life's work to him.

It meant I had to give Jesus my life and every major life-decision - of course, not the decisions which are too small to be of consequence; I mean, I had to surrender the driving seat of my life to him, and also, allow him to sit in the driver's seat of my life – to actually sit on the throne of my life, which was scary because everyone likes to be on control; but it made sense because if Jesus was all knowing and all powerful, he would do a much better job than me. Whatever words you use to explain it, "Give my life to Jesus" or "Let Jesus come into my heart" – the jargon is not important so much as your sincerity and trust (faith), but only when I was ready to give everything to Jesus, was the time that I knew that Jesus would be all or nothing; I realized that the Gospel according to Jesus was,

"Whoever wants to be my disciple must deny themselves and take up their cross daily and follow me. For whoever wants to save their life will lose it, but whoever loses their life for me will save it. What good is it for someone to gain the whole world, and yet lose or forfeit their very self?

Whoever is ashamed of me and my words, the Son of Man will be ashamed of them when he comes in his glory and in the glory of the Father and of the holy angels."
(Luke 9:23-26, New International Version Bible).

A total commitment and life-walk, an all-or-nothing commitment; it took me a few months of attending that Church and listening to sermons, but I knew that if I was to really be a Christian, I would follow him completely.

One day, a few weeks later, I woke up and said to myself, "Today's the day, I am finally ready." I was ready to hand over the reins of my life to Jesus. And when I did, it was like a huge weight lifting from me. Then and there, I said words to him, like, "Jesus, I now make you my Lord and Saviour. I give you my life. I ask you to come into my life, I give you all my burdens and years of living a lonely life without you. I repent of all my sins."

After my prayer of repentance, and giving God the reigns of my life, I opened my eyes and this new-found joy and amazing peace just welled up from within, and inside me I felt so clean and fresh, and outside everything felt so clean and fresh-like a newly born baby – it felt like I was starting my life all over again with a fresh, clean slate, wiped clean. Which, of course, in God's eyes, I was. I was also given a portion of the Bible from another lady in church called

Pauline, to place on my shelf, which read very aptly, "Therefore, if anyone is in Christ, he is a new creation: The old has gone, the new has come!"
(2 Corinthians 5:17, NIV Bible)

And I noticed this huge burden of worry I had been carrying around with me suddenly lifted and I felt so light and worry-free; this huge weight of oppression lifted from my shoulders – it was incredible – you have to experience it to believe it.

And for the next, at least, two years I felt like I was walking on air. And so began the greatest adventure of my life.

And that day that I actually gave my life to Jesus was when I felt I had started all over again – like a fresh, new baby, which spiritually I had become because my spirit inside me had been miraculously brought to life through the Holy Spirit reviving my dead spirit, which had laid dormant all my life. My life had been reborn and given a new lease of life. I had been reborn and now I knew what Jesus meant when he said, "You must be born again."
(John 3:7, NIV Bible)

And spiritually, this is what was happening because, in fact, my spirit had come to life – I was now regenerated because my Spirit was regenerated - what is called having a born-again experience; I also felt, gone were all the disappointments and days of trying to work out everything in my own strength because now I had an inner strength greater than Samson– the very real and most comforting presence of the Holy Spirit; my healing had begun. I now had a very real and tangible strength and a very presence I could turn to in times of trouble. I noticed other wonderful things too:

I noticed I had the strongest love in my heart or emotions which I could love my enemies with, because this love was the same love God loved me with, which is both an unlimited love and an unconditional love - it will never end and has no limits and cannot be measured (unlimited) and such a love is not merit-based (conditional) according to how well I performed but according to his unmerited love called "grace".

I now had a very present help residing in my emotions and heart that has proved to be the greatest source of comfort, healing, peace and joy for my life. And I invite you, today, to invite the greatest power of God's love to come into your life, too, and give you a tangible feeling of peace which will dispel all your fears.

And since that day 34 years ago, I have never ever looked back with regret. God has always proved to be faithful and pulled me through some of the most difficult and painful set of circumstances.

Maybe, you are thinking, "But I like to be in control of my life, and I definitely don't want to be one of those 'born again' religious freaks!", but, please, before you reject it, please experience for yourselves and see if Christianity is very real. You will never know unless you try. God says in his word, "Taste and see that the Lord is good! Oh, the joys of those who take refuge in him!"
(Psalm 34:8, The New Living Translation Bible)

Many people today have tried to find stability through riches and materialism – many politicians have promised us wealth by the pursuit of riches through "Capitalism" or "Materialism" but in the end these are just more empty promises, which are empty when we find all our hard work and investments have just run away with the wind of recession. In the end, we are just more messed up and full of worry and we need to hear Jesus' words who said,

"Come to me, all you who are weary and burdened, and I will give you rest. Take my yoke upon you and learn from me, for I am gentle and humble in heart, and you will find rest for your souls. For my yoke is easy and my burden is

light."
(Matthew 11:28-30, New International Version Bible)

Only when you actually experience God's love for yourself, when you invite God into your heart, and when God the Holy Spirit touches you by his grace, in spite of you not inviting him, then either way, the Holy Spirit will fill you with such an amazing peace, which alone can reach your deepest pain and hurt.

The process of becoming a Christian happens when God the Holy Spirit penetrates your spirit and touches you with a miracle so that you become born-again, but the ongoing revelation prior to this event and afterwards is a lifelong process of more and more revealing of Jesus Christ's grace. But you can start that process by praying the following two prayers. The first prayer is for those who are searching for truth and for the definitive answer, i.e. who want to know if God exists, and only an answer from God himself will satisfy their longing and quest. Therefore, asking God the prayer, "If you are all-powerful and you love me perfectly, then show me the power of this love and who you are" is really important as well as powerful.

I don't know if you have experienced the feeling of a peace from God the Holy Spirit ministering to you, ministering to you a peace which is so profound, it reaches and calms your fears, floods your mind and emotions with a tangible peace, but it is more ecstatic and joyous than I can imagine the feeling you get from smoking drugs. And of course, smoking drugs does a person a hell of a lot of harm, while receiving the joy and peace of God will only bring long-lasting healing, mental peace and well-being, both physically, emotionally and spiritually.

If you haven't experienced that for yourself, then please pray the prayers at the end of Chapter Two, and also read the following words from the Bible which is an invitation from God to invite you to test God's love for yourself personally. Because if you don't know or haven't experienced God for yourself, then you first need to test his love out for yourself.

Please read this invitation from the Bible in the book of Psalms:
"Taste and see that the Lord is good, blessed is the one who takes refuge in him."
(Psalm 34:8, New International Version Bible)

Do you want to receive this greatest comfort and hope in your life, which will be the greatest source of strength and joy in your heart and emotions?

Then, if you do, tell him you want to follow him because you are fed up with being so disappointed by following the world's way and your own thinking. Can I invite you to pray the following prayer:

The Seeker's Prayer:

"God,
I haven't always believed in you. I haven't known you. But I heard that you are a good God and that you are all-powerful - powerful enough to actually come into my life and show me who you are, and show me who I am in you, and who I could become in you; that you have the power to touch my heart – my spirit in such a way with your love that I become healed and whole, and my life is upgraded beyond my imagination.

Today, I want to experience your love for myself, your personal love in my life so that I realize you are not just God, but you are my very own Father who wants to adopt me as your own child into the family of God; and once I open my heart to you and take Jesus Christ as my personal Saviour - believe that he died for me on the cross and repent of my sins, then you will come in and touch my spirit and regenerate me and make me "born-again" as a new creation.

"I heard that you love me more than anyone I know, and that your love is so powerful, it will heal my every hurt and grief, and give me the greatest comfort, joy and the most profound peace in the deepest part of my life; please come into my heart and life and let the power of your love – the Holy Spirit – wash away all my pain, my sins, my griefs, which you bore on the tree of Calvary, please give me your perfect peace, now, as I wait in your blessed presence. I pray this prayer in faith. "

"I am sorry for following the world's way, but I decide to follow your way, please help me to believe in you by giving me your revelation and message through your Holy Spirit, that I am loved with your unlimited and unconditional love, by which I can love others who have hurt me and forgive them, and release them and me, forever."

"Please show me that you are alive and that your love is real for me. Please let me taste your love, let me experience the power of your love. Amen."

If you are ready to go further in God by actually receiving Jesus Christ as your own personal Saviour, and thus actually letting him adopt you into his family, whereby you become a child of God, and you believe Jesus died for you personally, then please pray the Sinner's Prayer.

You must repent of your sins and hand over the reigns of your life, sooner rather than later, you must repent and pray a prayer of repentance, i.e.

The Sinner's Prayer:

"Thank you, God that you sent your Son, Jesus Christ, to die for me, and when you died on the cross, you actually took all my sins as if I was the only person living who you died for alone, because even if I was the only person living on this Earth, you would have still come and died for me, personally, two thousand years ago. Thank you for that is how personal your love for me is."

"Dear Jesus, I believe that faith in your blood which you shed on the cross two thousand years ago cleanses me from all sin. I repent of all my sins, both intentional and unintentional, and the sins of not doing what we should do as well as doing things that we should not do."

"Thank you for your promise from the Gospel of John, which says that through believing in your saving name and receiving Jesus Christ into my spirit, I can be born-again and receive the promise of living with you for all eternity. As John wrote:

"He was in the world, and though the world was made through him, the world did not recognize him. He came to that which was his own, but his own did not receive him. Yet to all who did receive him, to those who believed in his name, he gave the right to become children of God— children born not of natural descent, nor of human decision or a husband's will, but born of God."

"Thank you, that you promised to adopt me now as your child, and as a guarantee of that sealing of adoption, you will send your Holy Spirit into my spirit as a seal. That you will anoint me and seal me with your precious Holy Spirit, who is the power of your love in action for me every day."

As Paul wrote,
"He anointed us, set his seal of ownership on us, and put his Spirit in our hearts as a deposit, guaranteeing what is to

come."

"Please come Holy Spirit and make me your own child, please place your seal in me, so I am sealed with your guarantee, your own precious child who has inherited all the inheritance of your Firstborn child. Please stay in me, living in my soul - in my mind, my emotions, my will and my spirit, continually giving me your precious and comforting peace, calming me and comforting me, and letting me continually commune with your Spirit, as you give me your continual perfect peace; please let your profound peace minister to me whenever I am afraid or whenever my mind needs calming. I want this greatest peace knowing that no one can snatch me out of your hands. So, I can finally have this peace with myself, my life, with other people and peace with you, God."

"Thank you, Jesus. In your name and for your glory, I pray. Amen."

(The first Bible reference from John 1:10-13, the second Bible reference from 2 Corinthians 1: 21-22, New International Version Bible)

Now bundle up all your guilt, shame, worries, hurts and

sins, even the unforgiveness and hate you may feel for other people, and place them into a rubbish bin (I don't mean you have to search for a literal rubbish bag, but imagine you are doing that – the important thing is that you decide to give up and surrender all your negatives at the greatest rubbish tip, called the cross) and pin those onto the back of Jesus at the cross, and release them to the greatest rubbish tip which is Calvary, and Jesus will release the greatest peace, love and comfort you will ever experience – maybe not instantly – but as you show him your faith and sincerity, a miracle will be born in your heart.

God's love for you is like a river which will wash away all your dirt and give you a peace and joy which comes from within – in time you will come to see and experience that – it will be your greatest source of joy and strength for you, everyday.

Jesus promises you from the Bible, in John, 7:37-39, "'If anyone is thirsty, come to me and drink. Whoever believes in me, streams of living water will overflow from within his belly.' By this he meant the Spirit, whom those who believed in him were later to receive.'"
(New International Version Bible)

When you ask Jesus to take over the throne of your life, he will give you joy and peace, nothing or no one can take away.

Remember: God always has the power to pull you through every and any situation, if you invite him into your life and trust him to take all your emotional pain and sin at the cross of Jesus Christ.

WOULD YOU LIKE TO RECEIVE REAL COMFORT IN A COMFORTLESS WORLD?

As we look around at this world, one thing is sure: it's getting darker and more desperate – people have placed their trust in politicians and those politicians have grossly disappointed them. For me, Jesus is my only comfort and hope in this comfortless and hopeless world. Place your trust only in him, who can never let you down. Maybe you feel as if God has let you down – maybe you have been through such intense suffering you wonder how a loving God can love you and allow such pain as well, but remember, his vision for us is so much wider than ours, and many times he uses suffering to make us more trusting of him.

Remember, when you feel as if life is too tough, God always has a purpose for everything you are going through; every seemingly trivial and painful trial is making you a person of character as you learn to trust his unfailing power and love. God's word tell us in Romans 8:28:

"And we know in all things God works for the good of those who love him, who have been called according to his purpose."(New International Version Bible)

Also, God's word tell us in Romans 5:4-5:
"We rejoice in our sufferings, because we know that suffering produces patience, and patience produces character; and character produces hope; and hope never disappoints us because God has poured out his love into our hearts by the Holy Spirit, whom he has given us."
(New International Version Bible)

This is how to receive the greatest peace, comfort and joy for your life. God's love for you is like a magnet that will draw you to him, and in time you will experience it as the greatest source of strength and healing for your life.

So at the age of nineteen, my eyes were opened to true reality and to the true truth - when I realized and knew that there is really, in God's eyes, no such concept of "my truth" or "your truth", which is a lie and distortion brought to us by outside dark forces, and inside self-deception but instead there is "the truth" which is God's reality, not a twisted reality according to our agenda. And there is also, The Truth, which is how Jesus referred to himself when he said these words,

"I am the way, the truth and the life."
(John 14:16, New International Version Bible)

And 1987 was the time the Spirit of God penetrated my heart of darkness - my spirit - with his light and revelation; and I realized then that this revelation was so powerful, it penetrated into my spirit and made my spirit come alive, my spirit which had laid dormant for so many years waiting for the Spirit of all spirits - the Spirit of all men and women and children to rest upon my spirit and breathe new life into me; and thus it opened my blind eyes to make the eyes of my heart and imagination truly come alive and see the real possibilities and enlightenment of what and how my life would really count for something great when the God of peace, love and comfort would enter my darkness and pain and elevate me to make my life count for something special and worthy of his reward.

Thus, during my nineteenth year of walking this Earth, I came to know who made me, who thought of me, who chose me to walk this Earth, but more than that, to let

Christ in me walk this Earth. I couldn't imagine this possibility until I prayed and asked Jesus to come into my heart, which means asking Jesus to give me his Spirit and let him come into my dormant spirit. Thus, starting a brand new relationship with your heavenly Father who is waiting for you to return to him and is stretching out his big arms of love, who is actually holding out his arms of love to you and me.

And in those thirty-four years, I have experienced him to be my one and only deliverer and comforter who can comfort me and reach the parts of me which no one else can reach. Who because he is God, he can reach my deepest pain and touch my needs where I need his love to assure me that he is in control. And because I have experienced God as someone who loves me more than anyone and has the power to heal me and flood my mind and emotions with a real and tangible peace, I can't begin to communicate to you how much your life will be upgraded when you come to not just know him but experience him.

When you come to that place at the cross when you want to relinquish all your worries and burdens and heaped-up stress and disappointments to him, then you too can find true peace, comfort and breakthrough - the greatest comfort and peace to alleviate all your problems and you too will find him to be the greatest source of well-being and health and peace for your mind, your body, your emotions, and the greatest rock and anchor for your spirit.

Most people want to upgrade their lives, I don't know anyone who doesn't. Most of us want to be more enlightened. Many of us want a more spiritually satisfying life. But do you know that in regard to spiritual enlightenment, we need our spirits and our spiritual antenna to first be repaired before that enlightenment can do its work of revelation, because we are all born with spiritual antennas which are broken and blocked?

Chapter Three.

How To Incline Your Life and Heart To God.

This chapter will continue on the subject of how to open yourself up to your spiritual possibilities which, you may never have imagined was possible before until you inclined your heart towards your father in heaven and towards the greatest knowledge of his personal love for you.

I don't know whether you know that there is a Father of all fathers who knows you more than anyone, who loves you more than anyone, and wants to have the most exciting and closest relationship with you built on faith.

Of course, we can't see him, but we can feel him - we can feel the activity of his Spirit moving upon us, yet, how can we discern him unless we ourselves have been born of his Spirit by our spirit being awakened so our antennas or spiritual receivers are repaired and re-tuned into the voice of God, which everyone who is born into this world has lost because of all humans have inherited the curse of the fallen and corrupted nature of humanity and this world brought by man's rebellion to God, whether that be passive rebellion or active rebellion. But when we receive Jesus Christ into our hearts by his Holy Spirit, then a miracle occurs in our heart and we become born again.

And if you struggle in your faith to believe, then God can help you and impart to you a measure of faith so that you will no longer find it difficult to believe.

Just as the Bible says,

"But because of his great love for us, God, who is rich in mercy, made us alive with Christ even when we were dead in transgressions—it is by grace you have been saved. And God raised us up with Christ and seated us with him in the heavenly realms in Christ Jesus, in order that in the coming ages he might show the incomparable riches of his grace, expressed in his kindness to us in Christ Jesus. For it is by grace you have been saved, through faith—and this is not from yourselves, it is the gift of God— not by works so that no one can boast. For we are God's handiwork, created in Christ Jesus to do good works, which God prepared in advance for us to do."

(Ephesians 2:4-10, NIV Bible)

Do you see those words, "..it is the gift of God"? Yes, you can receive, today, the gift of faith, and if you are not ready to believe, today, you can still receive by faith; and then, God the Holy Spirit will definitely impart a special faith to your spirit sooner or later, when you are ready; and you will be empowered in your life when you receive enough faith and revelatory faith to believe in Jesus Christ.

As we read above, God will enrich your life because he is rich in mercy and grace. And remember, those two words, grace and mercy mean very different actions from God our Father, but they are both from his deep motive of kindness to give us uncountable gifts. Mercy means "Not having what you do deserve", i.e. punishment for all the times we lied, stole or misrepresented God and ourselves and others; while grace means, "Having what we don't deserve, i.e. all or any of God's gifts".

And when we receive God's unlimited love and grace into our hearts, it means we will be empowered to love through his imparted love. I know after I became a Christian, suddenly I was able to love all those people who had hurt me, once I chose through my will, not my feelings to forgive them. And then I realized, in astonishment, that with God's love in my spirit, I could love all my once enemies or those who I once resented through his unlimited and unconditional love; and therefore, all hate was neutralized, and I was set free as I set them free in my spirit. And I'm sure somebody reading these words has also had people who have hurt them who they need to set themselves free of all that toxic hate, which hurts you more than them because it creates havoc and toxins in our emotions, mind and even can affect our physical as well as mental health.

So, After you become born-again, then you can start a fantastic and new relationship with God the Holy Spirit which will prove to you to be the greatest adventure of your life because when you live your lives to please God first, he promises to meet all your needs, as well as some of your wants, as we pray to him, just like the first Apostle to the Gentiles, i.e.the first evangelist who preached the Gospel (Gospel = Good news) of Jesus Christ to non-Jews, who wrote and prayed this prayer, in the Letter to the Ephesian Church,

"For this reason I kneel before the Father, from whom every family in heaven and on earth derives its name. I pray that out of his glorious riches he may strengthen you with power through his Spirit in your inner being, so that Christ may dwell in your hearts through faith. And I pray that you, being rooted and established in love, may have power, together with all the Lord's holy people, to grasp how wide and long and high and deep is the love of Christ, and to know this love that surpasses knowledge—that you may be filled to the measure of all the fullness of God."

"Now to him who is able to do immeasurably more than all we ask or imagine, according to his power that is at work within us, to him be glory in the church and in Christ Jesus throughout all generations, for ever and ever! Amen." (Ephesians 3:14-21, NIV Bible Version)

Did you notice from the above truths that we just read, that God is able to do immeasurably more than we could even ask for in prayer or imagine?

WOW!

Imagine that, that God can do more than we can ask or even imagine!
Maybe, if you are not, as yet, a believer, then, this could be too much of a stretch of your imagination. Or, if you are beginning to believe, does that truth not give you the feeling or physical impartation from God that he is strengthening and upgrading your faith, or if you don't feel that, then in time as you trust in him, you will, and your life will be truly

upgraded.

I know that everyone who walks along this path of life is trying to upgrade themselves? I don't know anyone who wants to downgrade themselves, even individuals who want to leave this world are looking for something better. But do you know that there is a possibility of upgrading your life far greater and more precious than you could ever have imagined?

If you haven't yet grasped the truth that there is someone who wants to take hold of you and pour such amazing gifts of love and peace, comfort and relief into your life, when you begin to trust him; then please invite him to do that at the end of this chapter, where you can pray the prayer called "The Sinner's Prayer" which is an alternative Sinner's Prayer from the prayers in Chapter Two.

ALL OF US WANT TO MAKE OUR LIVES COUNT, AT LEAST MOST OF US.

All of us are on different paths of life yet all of us are trying to make our life count for something - to try and make sure our lives are worth more than mere dust and earthly considerations and to find that something of much more noble and precious worth. To enable us to lift our eyes from thinking that we are merely earthen vessels of clay to finding the truth that we were made for something more glorious and that our destiny is to show that glorious revelation - to reveal the character of God and his unending and unconditional love, and particularly the amazing character of his Son of God-incarnate who displayed amazing character traits and endurance to pain in the name of his personal love for you, when he went to the cross and died the death of a criminal, in the name of his personal love for you, so that he would have still given his life for you even if you were the only person living on this Earth.

This book is about reminding us of that, despite what most of us learned at school when we were told that we are the culmination of a long line of millions of mistakes or mutations in lines of DNA over millions of years of genetic accidents, which nature favoured to enhance us into a better species from mere brutish animals of monkeys from insects, which developed into monkey-men, and then later, you and I; this book is about reminding us that that we are not just collections of atoms with electricity shooting through them, that we are not just mere physical bodies, but rather we are meta-physical individuals made by someone far nobler than nature because he is a Super-nature who knows all things and knows us better than ourselves; who exists apart from this physical world; which would explain where we received those meta-physical realities from we can observe within us - those "super-powers" or God-like powers which all of us have been endowed with - like our conscience which knows and tells us when we have just told a lie, when we have just stolen something or just done something so bad we need to reproach ourselves, like lying, stealing, fits of uncontrollable rage, or lusting in an adulterous way; when we have committed something which that power of re-approaching ourselves - our conscience - tells us in the light of God's standard of perfection, of which such knowledge cannot be revealed to us by mere atoms or mere molecules or surges of electricity; neither can they inspire or empower those other God-like faculties we also have within us like our self-consciousness and imagination which those creatures of the animal kingdom or the other creatures of lesser species of other kingdoms who are not born with such qualities of real-intelligence and real spiritual intuition like us humans are given to us by the King of kings from the Kingdom of kingdoms.

AS FOLLOWERS OF CHRIST, WE ARE ALL BEING CHANGED INTO HIS LIKENESS, FROM ONE LEVEL OF GLORY TO ANOTHER.

This book was written to help remind us who we are - that we are worth more than the dust and clay of this Earth because we were made to show and reflect the glory of God - and in Christ, we are gradually being transformed into his character and glory by his Spirit working in our deepest character and mind. That we are not, in spite of what we were taught at school, the end result of a long stream of accidents in nature which mother-nature or the forces of evolution selected those mutations in our ancestors of spiders and monkeys etc. - to develop them - our so called more brute ancestors of spiders and monkeys etc.- our Grandparents who were spiders and monkeys to develop them into monkey-men and then by some "miracle" deposited those God-like meta-physical faculties such as a conscience, a self-consciousness so they develop into human beings like us - nature's better developed species more suited to survive against the competition of survival of the fittest - you and me, a work-in-process; which personally, I don't believe in such a World-view called organic evolution or Darwinian evolution. Of course, I believe we are a work-in-process but it is the Spirit who is changing us gradually, as we surrender to his work.

In other words, although I don't believe in organic evolution, I do believe in a far more glorious evolution - God's spiritual, super-organic, evolution which carries far more hope and comfort for change which is through receiving the Spirit of Christ into our spirits and making us a new creation from man-oriented and worldly orientated individuals to God-orientated individuals. That you and I are made for something much better than to just grace this earthly abode for seventy, or eighty, or if we are lucky, ninety years, but rather, we are made to show God's unlimited, unconditional and unconquerable love, and to allow God's Spirit to enter our spirit and gradually evolve us, not into a vessel of clay on Earth, but a vessel fit for the Master in heaven; who not only is a God but who was tested in every way as a God-Man, who is Jesus Christ, who wants to give us not only God-like qualities - qualities we may have longed to have like the gods of the Greeks, but something much better, which they never had which is the power to overcome all our corrupted and corruptible human natures through the life and death of that God-man, Jesus Christ's Spirit filling our bodies and spirits and renewing them, by the Holy Spirit.

If you studied about the so called "gods" of the Greeks you will know that they were not gods because they did not possess the power to quell their own lusts of their sinful nature, their weaknesses, and their own spirit; of course, we know that they were only legends made by mere men; yet, only in Christ can we enjoy such a freedom, who crucified our old, human nature, and selfish and vulnerable self at the cross, and by the Spirit made us alive with him, who is now living in our spirits and renewing our minds and body everyday.

That's right, according to the Bible, we share in his crucifixion - not literal but spiritually, in that our old, sinful self, which is prone to make mistakes and sometimes lie and misrepresent the truth according to our whims or fears, can be neutralized through considering it crucified with Jesus.

As the Bible says,
"I am crucified with Christ, and I no longer live, but Christ lives in me. The life I live in the body, I live by faith in the Son of God, who loved me and gave himself for me."
(Galatians 2:20, New King James Version Bible)

And we not only share in his sufferings in this way, but we can also share in his glory.

Not that we ever share in God's omni-presence (his all-pervading presence) or his omni-potence (his all-powerfulness), but we will definitely share in his omniscience (his all-knowing) as is stated in the Bible,

"Now we see but a poor reflection as in a mirror; then we shall see face to face. Now I know in part; then I shall know fully, even as I am fully known."
(1 Corinthians 13:12, NIV Bible)

According to this Scripture, when we meet the Lord after we pass from this life, we shall know all things, including who God is, as well as who we are in him; and then we shall no longer know in part, but instead know all things; so it looks like we shall know everything, without being Mr. or Mrs. Know-it-alls!

Also, in John's letter,
"How great is the love the Father has lavished on us, that we should be called children of God! And that is what we are!
The reason the world does not know us is that it did not know him. Dear friends, now we are children of God, and what we will be has not yet been made known. But we know that when Christ appears, we shall be like him, for we shall see him as he is. All who have this hope in him purify themselves, just as he is pure."
(1 John 3:1-3, NIV Bible)

This is our hope which purifies us: We shall be like him, knowing all things without being all Know-it-alls, since we will be also humble and contrite, meek and mild as we will share in the same character of Jesus, which he would have transformed into us by his Spirit on this Earth, as he would have purged out all the dross through him crucifying our old sinful nature or prone-to-weaknesses and the weakness of our fleshly lusts and desires, as he has already and is working out, now, in our stubborn nature, and is also working out in us the character of Jesus Christ, as he is doing, now, here on Earth, as he has promised to do, from his words here, which is a promise in the Bible,

"And we, who with unveiled faces, all reflect the Lord's glory, are being transformed into his likeness with ever increasing glory, which comes from the Lord, who is the Spirit."
(2 Corinthians 3:18, NIV Bible)

WOW! This makes me want to shout, "WOW!" from the rooftops!

That everyday, God the Holy Spirit is working out in us - in our deepest beings as we let him - crucifying our old nature and transforming his new nature through my faith in him and his faith in me.

For as the Bible tells us,
"For it is God who works in you both to will and to do for His good pleasure."
(Philippians 2:13, NIV Bible)

Let me read that Scripture from Galatians 2:20, again,

"I am crucified with Christ, and I no longer live, but Christ lives in me. The life I live in the body, I live by faith in the Son of God, who loved me and gave himself for me." (Galatians 2:20, New King James Version Bible)

This is all part of the message of the Gospel and actually the greatest good news for men and women and children called the mystery of God made known to us through Jesus Christ's Spirit coming down to us and transforming our lowly bodies and making God and us united into a new man; who is enlightened with God's truth by his Spirit who can now overcome all the previous weaknesses and fallacies and other traits of his old, sinful, vulnerable to weaknesses lusts, and instead become a new man who now reflects God's knowledge, glory, and his unlimited love for his fellow.

And so, again, the message of the Gospel in a nutshell is this from the Bible,
"I am crucified with Christ, and I no longer live, but Christ lives in me. The life I live in the body, I live by faith in the Son of God, who loved me and gave himself for me." (Galatians 2:20, New King James Version Bible)

This is something which the forces of darkness - if you believe in that - or even better, if you believe in the devil of darkness, who has tried to steal away and rob all of us of that greatest knowledge we could ever find which is of more worth and more powerful and precious than all the gold of this world; of the greatest and noblest and treasured knowledge of who you and I are in relationship with that Spirit of all spirits. And that Spirit of all spirits who is actually the Maker of all men's spirits who I call "God", who wants to have a relationship with you in order for you to take your eyes off limited and earthly considerations and so elevate yourself to the most noblest and enlightening and empowering knowledge that you are loved by a Father in heaven who is longing to shower you and longing to have a relationship with you based on faith; who is waiting and longing, just like the Prodigal Son's Father in the Bible (Luke 15:11-32) who waits every evening for his long-lost son to return to his bosom, to enable you to lift up your eyes from mere limited concerns and instead consider, imagine and grasp the greatest knowledge you can learn and receive which is that God loves you personally, and unconditionally and unlimitedly in such a personal love that even if you were the only person living, he would have still come to this Earth and died for you.

Thus, God wants you to take your eyes off mere worldly matters and concerns and mere earthly, limited considerations, and look up and see and feel his amazing personal love for you, so that you would have the faith and power by his gifting of undeserved grace and mercy; so that we would believe supernaturally and the eyes of our understanding would be enlightened to know him, and know who we are in him, to give him all our worries, to relinquish all our stress, strain and pain and give them to Jesus Christ who is well able to take them; and instead be filled with his Spirit and tangible comfort and peace, every day; for when he died, he received and took everything which stands between you, and then, Jesus crucified them all with him, nailing them all to the cross; therefore, although the Devil thought he had accomplished victory over Jesus at the cross, it was Jesus' finest hour because what he did was took all those negatives which stand between you and God and nailed them to the cross; listen to this:

From the Letter of Paul to the Colossian Church,
"When you were dead in your sins and in the uncircumcision of your sinful nature, God made you alive with Christ. He forgave us all our sins, having cancelled the written code with all its regulations (i.e. the law of Moses), which stood against us and condemned us; he took it away, nailing it to the cross. And having disarmed the powers and authorities, he made a public spectacle of them, triumphing over them by the cross.
(Colossians 2:13-15, NIV Bible. Parenthesis by C.J. Briscoe)

Jesus' death and subsequent resurrection from the dead means that he has reclaimed the power of death and hell from the Devil; therefore, death and hell no longer have power over us, as long as we apply his death and resurrection to our own lives; once we do that, then we no longer need to fear death and fear the afterlife because it will be eternal life with Jesus for those who have placed their trust and eternal destiny in him. That's why Jesus took the keys of death and hell off the devil - meaning the authority of hell and death has been handed back to Jesus; so that now we can live a new, born-gain life without death again, with the same Spirit that raised Jesus from the dead living in our spirit, with the same power and love to raise our lowly bodies and minds into a new body of spiritual men and women of great, godly statue; thus, we can now hand over to God our heavenly father all our worries and burdens who wants to take away all your burdens and give us the greatest comfort and

RELIEF FROM ALL YOUR WORRIES,

so that you take your eyes off all your worries and place your trembling weak, tiny hand into the most powerful hands of love who is waiting to take hold of you and to steady you and guide into the greatest plan and most exciting adventure for your life of faith; to fill your mind and spirit with the greatest peace and comfort as you trust in him, and to inspire us to take our eyes of mere earthly considerations and to show each of us our potential great destiny in him, and enable us to walk in that destiny through his Spirit continually giving us more and more revelation of his personal love for us.

Jesus became the God-Man for us, forever, who eternally carries the wounds he suffered so that we don't need to suffer any more punishment; this God-incarnate we call Jesus Christ was literally fed to the wolves by his Father in heaven, even though us theologians say that Jesus is God the Son, and God is God the Father; although they are both one God but feeding your Son part of you to the wolves or feeding your Son to the wolves is more than mere nuanced considerations and the distinction we theologians make between God and his Son is important because it's more than just a nuanced or nominal difference - it's an important difference, namely between God-Sovereign and Son-Crucified, while his Father in heaven turned his back on him, for the sake of testing his Son to the limits; so that he was tested in every way as a man to ensure that God-Man was and is both fully Man and fully God, in order to unite in us both his Godliness with our humanness into a new Man of Jesus Christ in us; to restore all the Godly qualities back to us but now have something much better and powerful - which is the greatest mystery revealed to you and I - "God with us", living everyday in our spirit, so we can feel his power and unending love and commune with him by his Spirit. Not that we become gods but we are united with God, eternally, fellow-shipping with him.

Listen to this from the Apostle Paul, again from his Letter to the Colossian Church:

"I have become its servant by the commission God gave me to present to you the word of God in its fullness— the mystery that has been kept hidden for ages and generations, but is now disclosed to the Lord's people. To them God has chosen to make known among the Gentiles the glorious riches of this mystery, which is Christ in you, the hope of glory."
(Colossians 1:25-27, NIV Bible, italics by C.J. Briscoe)

So now, God's "endgame" or greatest vision for you and I is to restore all his Son's wonderful character of the risen, tested, tried and glorified Jesus, the Man-God in us, gradually, which is the true and greatest evolution - which is much a better BLUEPRINT than the first Adam, who although he was made in the image of God, he didn't have that God-Man, that enhanced new model of the new Adam inside him; which, you could say is bonus for us, to share in his glory, for his glory. That's why Jesus is also called "the new Adam" so we are sons, not of the old Adam, but of the new Adam, namely Jesus Christ.

And when he went to the cross and died for you personally, his shoulders are so big he took all your sin and the sins of the world upon his shoulders, and absolutely everything of negative forces of your life, including all the sicknesses and diseases and every pain and pathogen everyone has been terrorized by and there ever will try to take your peace away, and instead he has promised to give you the greatest peace, sense of security and greatest comfort you could ever enjoy for the rest of your life; so that whatever you face of pain and trial, you will always have inside you his Spirit giving you a very real comfort and rest and peace in the midst of the deepest torment and trouble.

If you want to give Jesus Christ all your burdens and pains and receive from him the greatest adventure for your life, then please read the following promises of God of Jesus Christ's work of redeeming your life from the pit of sin, of death, loneliness and despair. Also, most importantly, please pray either or both of the prayers from Chapter Two, or pray the prayer at the end of this Chapter Three.

In the Bible, in the book written by the disciple John, we can read,
"He was in the world, and though the world was made through him, the world did not recognize him. He came to that which was his own, but his own did not receive him. Yet to all who did receive him, to those who believed in his name, he gave the right to become children of God—

children born not of natural descent, nor of human decision or a husband's will, but born of God."
(John 1:10-13, NIV Bible)

The above promise tells us that Jesus Christ came to his own people - the Jews - who rejected him as their Saviour, yet, to anyone - including both Jews and non-Jews (Gentiles) - who receives Jesus into their heart, who believes in his free gift of salvation, they can become children of God, born not of earthly seed but born of God through God's Spirit inside them making them born-again.

NOT A LITTLE UPSTART BUT THE SON OF GOD WHO CAN MAKE YOUR OLD SPIRIT BORN-AGAIN BY HIS SPIRIT.

As we read in the introduction or Preface to this book, the story of Nicodemus, that's why one man in the Bible called Nicodemus came to Jesus at night - he was from the Jewish ruling Council so he feared fellow Jews knowing he had visited Jesus who the Jews regarded as "a little upstart". He came to Jesus to ask about salvation.

Let's read about it again, in the book of John, in the Third Chapter of his Gospel,

'He came to Jesus at night and said to him, "Rabbi, we know you are a teacher who has come from God. For no one could perform the miraculous signs you are doing if God was not with him."

In reply, Jesus declared, "I tell you truly, no one can see the kingdom of God unless he is born again."
"How can a man be born when he is old?" Nicodemus asked. "Surely, he cannot enter a second time into his Mother's womb to be born!"

'Jesus answered, "Truly I say to you, no one can enter the Kingdom of God unless he is born of water and the Spirit. Flesh gives birth to flesh, but the Spirit gives birth to spirit. You should not be surprised at my saying, 'You must be born again'. The wind blows wherever it pleases. You hear its sound but you cannot tell where it comes from or where it is going. So it is everyone born of the Spirit."
(John 3:2-8, NIV Bible)

In the above story, Jesus is trying to explain to Nicodemus that the Holy Spirit makes a person's spirit born-again, but just like the wind, you cannot trace where he has come from or where he is going. Yet, to all who are longing for the Spirit's appearing and working in your heart, who believes in Jesus' offer of salvation that he died for you and took all your sins on the cross to make you clean, then you can invite his Spirit - Jesus into your heart and make you born again. Only when you become born-again will you understand this because this kind of spiritual truth is not revealed by human flesh or understanding but by the Spirit of God.

It means when we receive Jesus' Spirit into our spirit, we have been adopted by God as his own son with all the inheritance and favour bestowed upon his own Son, Jesus Christ, given to us; and "us" means both to male and female variants of "adopted sons"; and as a guarantee of that adoption, God has promised that he will seal each of us with his own seal of his Spirit, as His own deposit in each of us, guaranteeing what is yet to come.

As it says from the book Ephesians, Chapter One, which is a letter written by Paul, the Apostle of Jesus.

"In him we were also chosen, having been predestined according to the plan of him who works out everything in conformity with the purpose of his will, in order that we, who were the first to put our hope in Christ, might be for the praise of his glory. And you also were included in Christ when you heard the message of truth, the gospel of your salvation. When you believed, you were marked in him with a seal, the promised Holy Spirit, who is a deposit guaranteeing our inheritance until the redemption of those

who are God's possession—to the praise of his glory."
(Ephesians 1:11-14, NIV Bible)

Also, please listen to this which tells us the difference between the first Adam, or man, Adam and the new Man, or new Adam, Jesus Christ, i.e. the first is a physical being, the second a spiritual, from the First book of 1 Corinthians, Chapter Fifteen,

"If there is a natural body, there is also a spiritual body. So it is written: "The first man Adam became a living being"; the last Adam, a life-giving spirit. The spiritual did not come first, but the natural, and after that the spiritual. The first man was of the dust of the earth; the second man is of heaven. As was the earthly man, so are those who are of the earth; and as is the heavenly man, so also are those who are of heaven. And just as we have born the image of the earthly man, so shall we bear the image of the heavenly man."
(1 Corinthians 15:44a-49, NIV Bible)

If you want to receive Jesus Christ's Spirit into your spirit, so that He would make you born-again, then ask ask him through praying the following prayer which is called,

The Sinner's Prayer 2:

"God,
if you are truly the most powerful God and you love me
more than anyone enough to come into my heart and show
me a miracle of healing, then please do that, according to
this promise that you reward all those who diligently seek
him.

Jesus, I heard that you are the most powerful physician in
the world, who can, not only heal me physically, but also
mentally, and most importantly, spiritually; and even if I am
not healed physically on this earth, I know that one day you
will heal me totally, when you raise me up from my grave
and give me a new body, because your Spirit, now, will
come into my spirit and make me born again. I now repent
of my sins and all the things I have done wrong to you, to
others and to myself; and I ask for your forgiveness, as I
forgive all those I have had a grudge and resentment to, by
an act of my will; I believe that because you suffered and
died for me, you took my punishment on the cross, and
through faith in your blood you spilled for me, this cleanses
me from all guilt as well as a guilty conscience; and I
believe you were raised so that I can believe not only in
your redemption on the cross, but also your justification to
me from all my wrong-doing - by your justification of me,
through you - when you were raised from the dead, so I will
also be raised from the dead and live forever with you.

Now I confess you as my Saviour, my Lord, and my Loving Father who will fill me with your Holy Spirit when I ask; and I know you will continue to guide me into this wonderful adventure of the Christian life - which I am about to learn is the best life and the nearest to a perfect life anyone can live.

For which I am eternally grateful. Amen."

Now that you have prayed the above, "Sinner's Prayer," it is important for you to go to some fellowship or local church where you can hear more teaching about Jesus Christ and how to be filled with the Holy Spirit; and teaching on how you can be continually guided by him through both his written word - the Holy Bible called in the Greek language, 'logos' and his spoken word - the 'rhema' word, meaning the Greek word for a spoken and personal message for you.

So please join a local church which teaches on both these messages of God and teaches about being filled with the Holy Spirit, and all the gifts of God the Holy Spirit.

Who teaches the entire counsel of God from the Bible - the 'logos' as well as his 'rhema.'

Jesus inspired, through the Holy Spirit these words for you, when you are full of worry or fear:

"Do not be worried about anything, but in everything, by

prayer and petition, with thanksgiving, present your requests to God. And the peace of God, which is so profound and deep, will guard your hearts and your minds in Christ Jesus."
(From the Book of Philippians 4:6-7, from the Holy Bible, New International Version, with six words or one sentence updated to modern usage, i.e. "which is so profound and deep")

Chapter Four

The Best Thoughts For Starting Your Day are Thinking About His Love.

All of us struggle with how to get our day off to a good start. We wonder which is the best way to step out - or the best way to get out of bed today. I am sure you have heard the expression, "Put your best foot forward!" I am also sure you have heard it said, "Did you get out of bed the wrong way, this morning?" - which I hope no one ever asks you such a question.

Personally, the best thoughts I have found helpful are thinking about what kind of thoughts God thinks about me.

For example, if you look at the words in the Bible, you can find these words which tell you how much God thinks about you because of his great love for you.

It says in the book of Psalms which King David penned, inspired by the Holy Spirit,

"O Lord, you have examined my heart and know everything about me. You know when I sit down or stand up. You know my thoughts even when I'm far away. You see me when I travel and when I rest at home. You know everything I do.

You know what I am going to say even before I say it, Lord. You go before me and follow me. You place your hand of blessing on my head. Such knowledge is too wonderful for me, too great for me to understand!...............
How precious are your thoughts about me, O God. They cannot be numbered! I can't even count them; they outnumber the grains of sand! And when I wake up, you are still with me!"
(Psalm 139:1-4 + 17-18, New Living Translation Bible).

As you begin your day, think about his immense love for you; Jesus said that when we pray to our Father in heaven, he knows what we need before we ask him.

Jesus said these words:
"When you pray, don't be like the hypocrites who love to pray publicly on street corners and in the synagogues where everyone can see them. I tell you the truth, that is all the reward they will ever get. But when you pray, go away by yourself, shut the door behind you, and pray to your Father in private. Then your Father, who sees everything, will reward you."

"When you pray, don't babble on and on as the Gentiles do. They think their prayers are answered merely by repeating their words again and again. Don't be like them, for your Father knows exactly what you need even before you ask him!"
(Matthew 6:5-8, New Living Translation Bible)

The next verse, in Verse 6, Jesus goes on to teach us what the Church calls, "The Lord's Prayer". You can read that prayer in Matthew 6:9-13. If you are a new Christian, I also recommend reading the Gospel of John first before you read the other disciples' Gospels, so that you can be acquainted with both the deity and the humanity of this God-Man, Jesus Christ; and also, the book of John was written for non-Jewish audience unlike the other Gospels, apart from Luke whose Gospel and his other book of "The Book of the Acts of the Apostles" was written for both Jews and Gentiles.

The best way to start your day off on the right track is to give God thanks and praise, even if you don't feel like it. This is called in the Bible by King David, "a sacrifice of praise."

How about praying this prayer daily before you start the day?

A Dedication Prayer to Start My Day Off on the Best Foot:

"Thank you God,
That you have chosen me to be at the center of your love

and will through the unmerited favour, i.e. grace of my Lord, Jesus Christ. I praise and worship you for your wonderful love and amazing grace to me today. Please give me opportunities to show that grace to others and to introduce that grace to others.

As I start this day, I know that the most important component and most empowering ingredient of my day is having you in my day, is having your presence in me as a shield protecting me, so that your very real and tangible Spirit of peace, comfort, protection and anointing would be upon me today.

Thank you, that I am surrounded by your protection and peace. Thank you that I am safe and secure with your everlasting arms under me.

I know that whatever happens today your love for me will enable me and empower me. That whenever trouble overtakes me, your love and power will equip me with the greatest sure-footing for my life. That whenever I feel scared or overwhelmed with anxiety, when I trust in you and pray to you, your Holy Spirit will give me your perfect peace. That there is nothing beyond your love and the power of your love to pull me back from the brink of hopelessness.

Thank you that when I trust you, I have a sure hope and anchor for my soul, and that you will never let me go.

Thank you, that you hold the highest, furthest and deepest parts of this universe in the palm of your hands, as well as me, and that you are not only the sovereign God of this universe, but you are the sovereign God of all my life as well as all my problems; I leave all of the worries and problems of my heart and mind in your capable hands, I am not able to deal with them, but I know you are more than able.

I thank you, Lord, that you love me with an unlimited love and an unconditional and perfect love; I thank you that your love is the answer to all of my problems; as well as you alone know the deepest recesses of my heart and soul, and only your Holy Spirit can reach my deepest pain and hurts to heal me, and give me peace, twenty-four hours a day. Whenever I face some obstacles today, please let me place my small hand in your big hand and place my small trust in your trusting arms of love, where I can be rest assured I couldn't be in a safer place, just like the dry and peaceful seagull perched under the cleft of a rock who has found the perfect spot. My perfect spot is in you, learning to trust you and lean on you, where I find a perfect peace.

And so whatever happens today, I know that nothing is going to happen today, that you and I cannot handle together, as you hold the solution to all my problems because you are always sitting on your throne.

So I ask you to come and be Lord of my life, my day, and everything that happens to me today.

I dedicate this day into your hands. There is nothing more that I want today than to see you pleased with my faith and honouring you; there's nothing more that I want than to see you glorified through my life, today. Help me to serve you alone, and to always look to your love and focus on you. Come Holy Spirit please glorify Jesus Christ through me, today.

I humbly ask that your blessed and comforting Spirit would be the most integral part of my day. Please anoint me and fill me with your blessed Spirit so that you would empower me today, and I would be filled with the knowledge of your love so that I would walk in your Spirit, continually guided by you and glorifying Jesus Christ, all day and every day.

Please fill me and equip me with your blessed anointing today. Please pour out your fresh anointing into my spirit and give me a fresh revelation of your love, as I wait upon you my. There is nothing more that I want than to please you and nothing more than to be filled with your blessed

Spirit today, so I can grow in my knowledge and experience of you and that others would also experience your blessed and comforting Spirit of grace.

Please give me a greater anointing as I seek your presence and your precious and most comforting anointing by your Holy Spirit, so that people who don't know you would see your love, and feel your presence in me; so that they would also come to know your love, personally for themselves, and be forgiven and find your wonderful peace and amazing grace. Please open up divine opportunities for me to share about your wonderful love and amazing grace and that I would be a vessel of your love, mercy and grace, so people would experience you through me, by your Spirit.

I only want to do your will today, so please show me how I can serve you and please you by walking guided by your Spirit. Please fill me afresh with your Spirit and the knowledge of your will and revelation for my life, so that I can live a life and a day pleasing you in every way, and bearing good fruit for you in the works you have called me to do.

Strengthen me by the power of your Spirit, and wherever I roam today, let me carry and impart your Holy presence so that people would feel your great love, and be convicted of their great need of you.

Please give me your peace, now, and healing and let me
be used as a vessel of your mercy, grace and healing. I
know your Holy Spirit is healing me, now. And when you
look at me, because I hold your Son, Jesus Christ in my
heart, you look at your Son in me, and I am perfect, in your
Son. You declare that I am your completely forgiven child,
and you declare that you have thrown all my sins into the
depths of the deepest ocean, i.e. that you have forgotten all
our sins so completely that they might as well be buried at
the bottom of an ocean. As your word says in the book of
Micah, Chapter 7, Verses, 18-19,

"Who is a God like you,
who pardons sin and forgives the transgression
of the remnant of his inheritance?
You do not stay angry forever
but delight to show mercy.
You will again have compassion on us;
you will tread our sins underfoot
 and hurl all our iniquities into the depths of the sea."

- so that in your mind, all our past sins are forgotten
through Christ taking our punishment at the cross so that
we are justified in your presence.

I thank you that you have adopted me into the family of
God, and sealed me with the seal of your Spirit,

guaranteeing all you have promised in the Bible, for now and for my glorious future with you.

Please guide me today in your perfect and wise will for my life; please go with me, today, wherever I roam, and give me your amazing peace, second by second, as I trust in you, as I release all of my worries and concerns into your hands; knowing you have promised that when I relinquish all of my concerns to you, you send your comforting Holy Spirit, to minister your greatest peace, comfort and remedy to my every emotion and all of my mind and spirit. Please come , Holy Spirit, and fill me with your power and grace, so I can be graceful and show your most powerful love to others, who need your love and remedy today.

This love which you promised us, will never fail, will never end, will never be broken. Help me to hear your still, small voice speaking to me and guiding me throughout this day, and fill me with your strength through your joy and peace ministering to me, and through me, all day long. Help me to make opportunities and give you the space and time to speak to me, by your still, small voice.

I pray that I can glorify you, today, through your Spirit, in my thoughts, as I focus on you, in all my activities, and speech.

In your name alone, I pray.

Amen."
(Bible Reference from Micah 7:19, New International Version Bible)

After you pray this prayer, have the faith – believe that His Spirit is now pouring himself into your spirit and emotions and preparing great things for your day, because you did the most important activity and best priority to start your day – which is to pray to your heavenly Father who knows what you need before you pray, who loves you more than anyone, who knows you more than anyone, who, alone thought of you as an idea, before time and space began. Who is your greatest remedy in this life of wonderful joy as well as suffering.

I hope you have found these words helpful in this book. If you need to contact me to ask me any burning questions please feel free to contact me with my contact details below.

Author's Contact:
Also, if you would like to know more how to receive Jesus Christ in your life, and everyday experience what it means to fellowship with him by the Holy Spirit, feel free to contact the Author at christinme@live.co.kr